kwjc

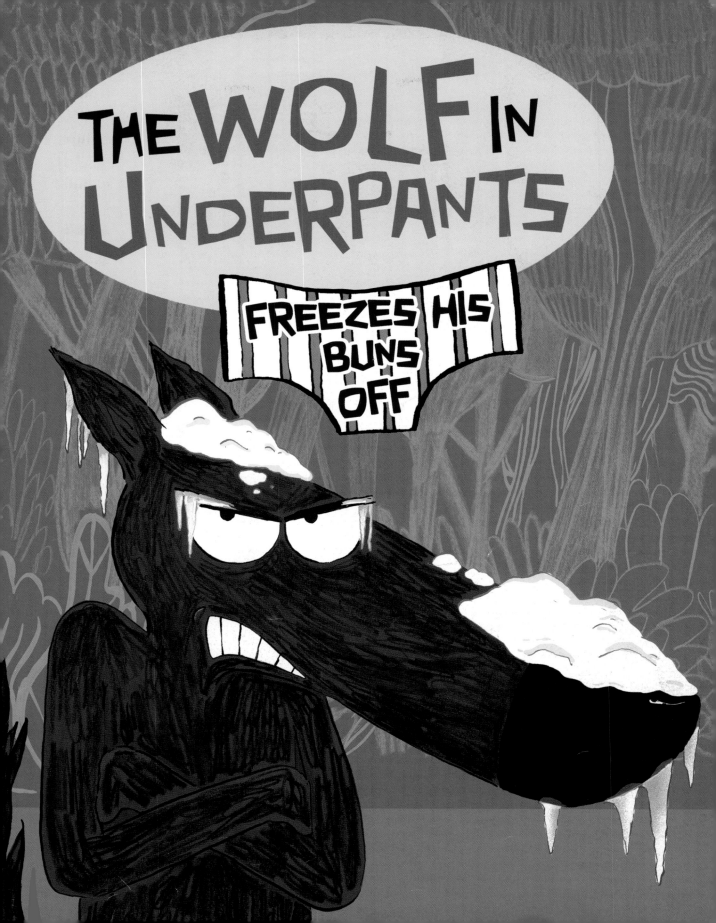

Story by Wilfrid Lupano
Art by Mayana Itoïz
With the friendly artistic participation of Paul Cauuet
Translation by Nathan Sacks

First American edition published in 2020 by Graphic Universe™
Published by arrangement with Mediatoon Licensing - France
Le Loup en slip se les gèle méchamment
© Dargaud Benelux (Dargaud-Lombard S.A.) 2017—Lupano, Itoïz, and Cauuet. All rights
reserved. Original artistic director: Philippe Ravon.
www.dargaud.com

Graphic Universe™
An imprint of Lerner Publishing Group, Inc.
241 First Avenue North
Minneapolis, MN 55401 USA

For reading levels and more information, look up this title at www.lernerbooks.com.

Main body text set in Stick-A-Round. Typeface provided by Pintassilgoprints.

Library of Congress Cataloging-in-Publication Data

Names: Lupano, Wilfrid, 1971- author. | Itoïz, Mayana, 1978- illustrator. | Cauuet, Paul,
    1980- illustrator. | Sacks, Nathan, translator.
Title: The wolf in underpants freezes his buns off / Wilfrid Lupano ; art by Mayana Itoïz and
    Paul Cauuet ; translation by Nathan Sacks.
Other titles: Loup en slip se les gèle méchamment. English
Description: Minneapolis : Graphic Universe, 2020. | Originally published in French by Dargaud
    Benelux in 2017 under title: Le loup en slip se les gèle méchamment. | Summary: When
    the wolf complains about the freezing-cold winter, the other forest animals fear he will
    return to his wild, evil ways.
Identifiers: LCCN 2019008576 | ISBN 9781541528192 (lb : alk. paper)
Subjects: LCSH: Graphic novels. | CYAC: Graphic novels. | Wolves—Fiction. | Forest animals—
    Fiction. | Winter—Fiction.
Classification: LCC PZ7.7.L86 Wq 2020 | DDC 741.5/973—dc23

LC record available at https://lccn.loc.gov/2019008576

Manufactured in the United States of America
1-44702-35533-8/13/2019

THE WOLF IN UNDERPANTS FREEZES HIS BUNS OFF

Wilfrid Lupano

Mayana Itoïz
and
Paul Cauuet

Graphic Universe™ • Minneapolis

WINTER HAS FALLEN WITHOUT
SO MUCH AS A SOUND. AND IN
THESE WOODS, WHEN THERE'S
SNOW ON THE GROUND, IT GETS
COLD AS ALL GET-OUT.

5

WOWZA! THESE SKIS ARE GREAT!

YOU KIDDING? I HAVE MY HEAVY-DUTY COAT.

AND TO WARM UP, WE EAT DELICIOUS CHEESE FONDUE.

DON'T FREEZE! CHEESE

CHEESE 50¢

CHEESE WAGON

SPLOOSH!

WHAT THE . . . ?
WHAT'S GOING ON!?

AND WHY ARE YOU
WEARING A SWIMSUIT?

HIS FEET!

HIS **FEET** ARE FREEZING! IT'S ALL THAT WALKING IN THE SNOW.

AAAH!!! OF COURSE!

LET'S ASK THE OWL TO KNIT HIM SOME SOCKS!

SOCKS? I'VE NEVER SEEN A WOLF IN SOCKS... SIGH... WELL, IF YOU INSIST...

AS THEY WAIT FOR THE OWL TO KNIT AN ENORMOUS PAIR OF SOCKS, THE ANIMALS ENJOY A BIG POT OF FONDUE, WITH A NICE STRING OF CHEESE FOR EACH OF THEM.

OH **YEAH!** FONDUE TIME!!!

WAIT, I LOST MY BREAD CUBE.

AND ONCE THE SOCKS ARE FINALLY FINISHED...

HEY, LITTLE GUY! WANT TO GET A REWARD? GO GIVE THESE SOCKS TO THE WOLF.

BUT ON A SNOWY NIGHT LIKE THIS, IT'S EASY TO GET LOST . . .

BRRR, I'M COLD. WHAT'S WITH THIS WINTER . . . AND WHERE IS THE WOLF?

NOTHING BUT SNOW ALL AROUND . . . AND IT'S ABOUT TO GET DARK . . .

HOPEFULLY I'LL FIND HIM TOMORROW . . . IT'S SO, SO COLD . . .

CAN YOU TELL ME WHAT
EXACTLY YOU'RE DOING?

STILL? WHAT'S WITH HIM?

DIDN'T HE GET THE SOCKS?

IF YOU ASK ME, THAT RABBIT NEVER FOUND THE WOLF.

WELL, I SAW EVERYTHING! THE BUNNY **DID** FIND THE WOLF. HE SAID THAT HE WAS REALLY COLD. AND THE WOLF REPLIED . . .

"YOU'LL BE NICE AND WARM IN MY BELLY!"

A HAT?

I'VE NEVER SEEN A WOLF
IN A HAT. BUT HEY, IF IT
HELPS YOU RELAX . . .

AND AS THE OWL
KNITS A HAT . . .

HEY! LITTLE BUDDY!

WANT SOME FONDUE? GO GIVE
THIS HAT TO THE WOLF.

AH, HE CAN HAVE HIS HAT TOMORROW. IT'S RIGHT HERE. I DON'T CARE ANYMORE . . . I'M **SO COLD!**

SUDDENLY . . .

OH?
DID YOU SAY COLD?

IT'S THE HAT! LOOKS LIKE THE LITTLE BOAR NEVER GAVE IT TO THE WOLF.

HE MUST HAVE GOTTEN SCARED. NOT VERY BOLD FOR A BOAR . . .

LISTEN, I WAS THERE! THE WOLF WENT, "DID YOU SAY COLD?"

"IN MY BELLY, YOU'LL NEVER BE COLD AGAIN!"

SLAM!

UH . . . WHAT'S UP?

GUESS WHAT HAPPENS? THERE ARE LOTS OF ANIMALS WHO DON'T KNOW WHERE TO LIVE. THEY FREEZE OUTSIDE. SO I INVITE THEM TO TAKE SHELTER HERE.

AH, I SEE. SO HE REALLY SAID, "YOU'LL BE NICE AND WARM IN MY **DWELLING.**"

PERFECT. JUUUSST PERFECT . . .

. . . CAN MAKE YOU LOOK **FRIGHTFUL!**

WITH FANGS LIKE ICE PICKS!

SO YOU'D BETTER ROLL YOUR CHEESE ON OUT OF HERE . . . AND GATHER UP YOUR HAZELNUTS . . .

OTHERWISE . . .

HOLD ON TO YOUR BUNS!

AFTER THIS WINTER MIX-UP,
EVERYONE IN THE WOODS
HAS TRIED A LITTLE HARDER
TO BE KIND TO OTHERS.
NOTHING'S PERFECT . . .

BUT IT'S A WARMER PLACE
THAN IT USED TO BE.

ABOUT THE CREATORS

WILFRID LUPANO

Wilfrid Lupano was born in Nantes, in the west of France, and spent most of his childhood in the southwestern city of Pau, France. He spent his childhood reading through his parents' comic book collection and enjoying role-playing games. He studied literature and philosophy, receiving a degree in English, before he began to script comics. He has written numerous graphic novels for French readers, including the series *Les Vieux Fourneaux* (in English, *The Old Geezers*). With this series, Lupano and Paul Cauuet first developed the idea that would become *The Wolf in Underpants*. Lupano once again lives in Pau after spending several years in the city of Toulouse.

MAYANA ITOÏZ

Mayana Itoïz was born in the city of Bayonne, in the southwest of France, and studied at the institut supérieur des arts de Toulouse (School of Fine Arts in Toulouse), where she worked in many different mediums. In addition to being an illustrator and a cartoonist, she has taught art to high school students. She lives in the Pyrenees, near France's mountainous southern border, and splits her time between art, family, and travel.

PAUL CAUUET

Paul Cauuet was born in Toulouse and grew up in a family that encouraged his passion for drawing. He was also a fond reader of classic Franco-Belgian comics such as *Tintin* and *Asterix*. He studied at the University of Toulouse and went on to a career as a cartoonist. Cauuet and Wilfrid Lupano first collaborated on an outer-space comedy series before working together on *Les Vieux Fourneaux* (*The Old Geezers*).